MAGGIE THE TALENTED MOUSE

Story by

John E. Becker, Ph.D.

Illustrations by

Keith W. Knore

*To Aubrey
Very talented indeed!
John Becker*

ISBN:9781521514665

To my grandson Maddox, who is "very talented indeed."

- John

To my wife, Brenda, for her enduring support, encouragement and patience during the illustration of Maggie's journey. Thank you, my love.

- Keith

With special thanks to Brandon Becker

*

Maggie the Mouse sat in the warm morning sunlight thinking about the terrible day she had at school the day before.

Her teacher, Mrs. Ratimore, told the children that they could share a special talent they had with the class on Monday. All the children were very excited – that is all the children except Maggie.

Of course, Frieda Field Mouse was excited, because she had a beautiful singing voice. And Charlie Church Mouse could juggle five acorns at one time. Even little Mary Meadow Mouse could recite the poems she had written.

But what could Maggie do? She had no talent at all, and by Monday, everyone would know it!

She simply had to find something she could do that no one else could.

Suddenly, she had a brilliant idea, "I'll learn how to fly! That's something no other mouse can do!"

But who could teach a mouse to fly?

"Horatio Horned Owl!" she exclaimed as the solution to her problem became perfectly clear. "I'm absolutely, positively, 100 percent sure that he can show me how to fly!"

Maggie scurried across the forest floor until she came to the gnarled old tree that Horatio called home.

"Oh, my!" she muttered when she spied the fearsome looking owl in the hollow of the tree. "How should a mouse go about asking an owl for help?"

"VERY CAREFULLY!" she decided.

"What am I afraid of, he's only an . . . owl," she gulped.

Maggie hesitated just long enough to steady her wobbly legs, and then she whispered in a mousey little voice, "Horatio."

The owl didn't stir at all.

So, Maggie took a deep breath, gathered up her courage, and squeaked with all her might, **"HORATIO!"**

As the great horned owl slowly opened one eye, and then the other, Maggie scampered up the tree.

"Horatio," she sputtered, "you've got to teach me how to fly. Everyone has a talent but me, so if you could teach me to fly, I . . . "

"Excuse me, my dear," Horatio said as he hopped out of his tree staring at Maggie through hungry eyes. "I'm afraid you don't understand. Normally, owls don't help mice . . . they usually . . ."

"Yes, yes, I know all that," Maggie said impatiently, "but this is different."

"Regardless," Horatio interrupted her, "even if I wanted to help you, aren't you forgetting something?"

"I don't think so," Maggie replied.

"You have no feathers," Horatio pointed out an obvious fact.

"Feathers?" Maggie said in a surprised voice, "what do feathers have to do with it?"

"Well, for one thing, you can't very well fly without them," Horatio said sleepily.

"Oh," Maggie said, a little embarrassed to have overlooked such an important detail.

Before Maggie could think of anything else, Horatio was fast asleep again.

Now what can I to do? She thought to herself. Then she had another idea. "Barney Beaver!" she cried. "I'm absolutely, positively, 100 percent sure that he could teach me how to swim. Then I would be the only one in my class who could!"

When Maggie arrived at the peaceful blue-green pond on the edge of the forest, she called to Barney.

Barney swam to the shore, and waddled over to where Maggie was waiting. Without taking a single breath, Maggie explained her urgent need for swimming lessons.

"I can't stop now," Barney replied gruffly. "I've got a lodge to build!"

"What if I helped you? If I saved you some time, you could take a few minutes off to teach me how to swim like a beaver."

"Maggie . . ." Barney began.

"Pleeeese," she begged with big, pleading eyes.

"Oh, okay, start dragging some of those branches down to the water."

Maggie was as happy as a mouse could be. She quickly found a branch and tried to move it, but it wouldn't budge. Then she tried a smaller branch, then another, and another, until she found one small enough to handle. It was hard work, but she finally managed to get it to the pond.

When Barney swam back to shore and saw the size of Maggie's branch, he frowned.

"Is that the best you can do?" he demanded.

"Well . . . yes," Maggie admitted.

"That's not going to save me any time at all," he snapped. "Besides, look at that skinny, little tail of yours. You need a big, wide tail like mine if you are going to swim like a beaver."

And without another word, Barney went back to work leaving Maggie to ponder her next move.

Maggie was a little discouraged, but she wasn't the kind of mouse to give up easily. "I've just got to think of something else," she said determinedly.

Just then, she spotted an ant. Perfect! She thought. Ants are great at building things, and I'm absolutely, positively, 100 percent sure that they could teach me how to build a house!

Maggie quickly explained her problem to the ant.

"We're awfully busy," the ant pointed out. "We've got to finish the entrance to our new home before the rains come."

"I can help you!" Maggie squeaked excitedly.

"Well, I'm not so sure . . ." the ant began.

"Just give me a chance, I'm sure I can be a big help!" Maggie said confidently.

   The little ant thought for a moment. Then he motioned for Maggie to follow him to the ant's new home.

The little ant introduced Maggie to the other ants, and explained her offer. The ants looked doubtful, but agreed to let her try.

Being surrounded by so many ferocious looking insects made her a little nervous, but Maggie was determined to help the ants so they would help her.

"Push that sand over here," the little ant directed Maggie.

Eager to make a good impression, Maggie stuck her nose in the sand and pushed with all her might.

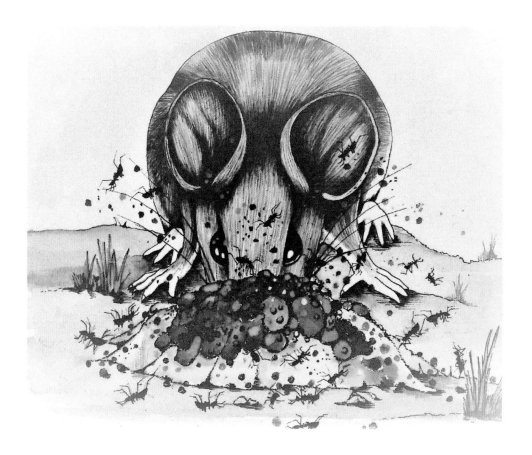

Suddenly, there were ants running everywhere shouting, "GO AWAY! GO AWAY!"

As the furious ants tried to repair the mess she had made, Maggie slipped quietly away.

For a few moments, she sat by herself, fighting back the tears.

"I'm just not talented at all," she moaned. "I'm, sniff, absolutely, sniff, positively, sniff, 100 percent sure that I'll never be talented at anything."

All at once, the afternoon calm was shattered by the sound of hissing and growling, and loud, angry voices.

Maggie hurried toward the stream where all the commotion was coming from.

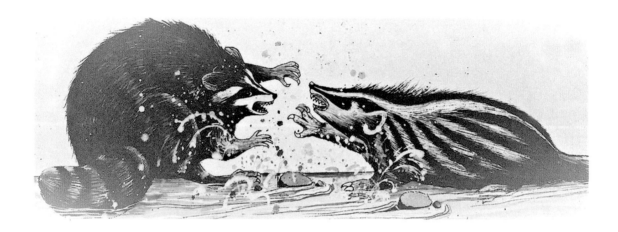

When she got there, Benjamin Badger and Ricky Raccoon were having a terrible fight.

Once again, Maggie plucked up all her courage and squeaked as loudly as she could, "STOP FIGHTING THIS INSTANT!"

Ricky and Benjamin stopped clawing at each other and peered in Maggie's direction.

"What are you two fighting about?" Maggie asked.

"I found Benjamin in MY fishing spot," Ricky hissed.

"You don't own the stream," Benjamin snarled. "I've got just as much right to that spot as you do!"

"No, you don't!"

"Yes, I do!"

"You don't!"

"I do!"

"Boys, boys," Maggie squeaked above the din. "Rather than fighting, why don't you try helping each other, and I'm sure that you'll find enough food for both of you."

"That would never work," Benjamin said shaking his head, "because Ricky would never share."

"Of course, I would!" Ricky fumed, his fur a little ruffled by the mere suggestion that he wouldn't be willing to share.

"There, it's settled!" Maggie proclaimed. "Now, you can stop fighting and be friends again."

Following Maggie's suggestion, Benjamin and Ricky waded into the stream.

Before long, they were busy helping each other dig up lots of food.

They were so busy, in fact, that they didn't notice Maggie disappearing into the shadows of the forest.

Maggie was pleased that Benjamin and Ricky were friends once again, but it would soon be dark, so she began trotting for home.

She hadn't gone very far when she heard the familiar voice of Horatio Horned Owl from the trees above.

"It takes a special talent to do what you just did," he said with a smile.

"It does?" Maggie said. "But I really didn't do anything."

"Oh, yes you did," Horatio insisted. "You were able to help those two settle their disagreement without fighting, and anyone who can do that is very talented indeed!"

As Maggie continued down the path, she thought about what Horatio said, ". . . very talented indeed!"

"I just knew that I had a special talent. I was absolutely, positively, 100 percent sure that I did!"

Dr. John E. Becker is an author of 26 Children's Books including his fictional picture book, Mugambi's Journey, his Best-Selling book, Frenemies for Life, the award-winning book, Wild Cats Past & Present, the Returning Wildlife series, and eight Seedling books. He is a graduate of The Ohio State University, a former elementary school teacher, college professor at Macalester College and the University of Florida, administrator at the Columbus Zoo, and he worked in the field of wildlife conservation for many years. Dr. Becker lives in Deerfield Beach, Florida, and has taught writing at the Thurber House Literary Center in Columbus, Ohio, for the past twenty years. You can contact Dr. Becker through his website: www.johnbeckerauthor.com.

Mr. Keith W. Knore has illustrated 3 books, is a graduate of The Columbus College of Art & Design and The Ohio University. He worked as artist and Art Director at WOSU-TV where he won 2 Emmy Awards for TV Show Open and Scenic Design from the National Academy of Television Arts and Sciences. He worked as Creative Art Director for a computer graphics company and taught Commercial Art at the Tolles Career and Technical Center where he was awarded membership to The National Technical Honor Society for outstanding teaching service. Mr. Knore lives in Columbus, Ohio with his wife Brenda of 50 years and their two Schipperke's Drummer and Champ.

Made in the USA
Columbia, SC
22 January 2019